THE
TOUCAN
BROTHERS

First published 2013 by Macmillan Children's Books
This edition published 2015 by Macmillan Children's Books
an imprint of Pan Macmillan
20 New Wharf Road, London N1 9RR
Associated companies throughout the world
www.panmacmillan.com

ISBN: 978-1-5098-0139-8

Text and illustration copyright © Tor Freeman 2013
Moral rights asserted.

1 3 5 7 9 8 6 4 2

A CIP catalogue record for this book is available from the British Library.
Printed in China

For Richard,
a big part of
the story.
T.F.

THE TOUCAN BROTHERS

Tor Freeman

MACMILLAN CHILDREN'S BOOKS

When your loo's got the blues

and the shower's run dry,

When the sink's on the blink

and the soap's in your eye.

When you're wearing the cushions to cover your ears,

To drown out the tap that's been dripping for years.

In Tapton everyone knows who to call . . .

The fast-plumbing toucans, Sammy and Paul!

For a splish or a splash they'll be there in a flash,
For a drip or a drop they will come on the dash.

Sammy and Paul have the plungers and spanners,
They have the know-how and impeccable manners!

For a job you can't do, just call those who can,
The twosome that can do: the Brothers Toucan!

Who finds Giraffe that
one extra metre?

And who installs Anteater's
swanky new heater?

Who will tell Mole
that his tap wasn't on?

And who will discover
where Pig's boot has gone?

And when the job's done and they're certain they've fixed it,
Who will have tea with a chocolate biscuit?
The answer is easy – it's Sammy and Paul,
For no job is too big and no pipe is too small.

One afternoon at the brothers' HQ,
The emergency phone rang (the red, not the blue.)

On the line was the Mayor, quite in a pickle,
The spout from his fountain reduced to a trickle.

The birds arrived quickly with ladder and tools,
And a well-thumbed edition of *Good Plumbing Rules*.
But as they were working they spied a van driving,
With letters announcing NEW PLUMBER ARRIVING!

The van pulled to a stop and a crowd gathered round,
And out jumped a hat-wearing, tool-toting hound.

He had gadgets that whirred, and things that went beep,
And he guaranteed all of his prices were cheap.

"I'm top of the pipes, and plumbing's my game,
Call me – whenever! Flash Rover's the name."

Paul felt downhearted but Sam said, "Don't fear!
We've been honing our plumbing craft year after year.
We're honest and good and we do what we say.
This dog may be cheaper, but better? No way!"

But soon the birds' work had completely dried up,
All of their customers pinched by that pup!

Come a spurt or a spout and that dog was about,
And when something burst, he was always there first.

Seems folk are just smitten by anything new.
The birds were left jobless, with nothing to do.

But what Paul didn't know and what Sam didn't guess,
Was that this cheeky mutt was just making a mess!

He'd seal up a crack using any old thing,
He'd tie boilers together with big balls of string!

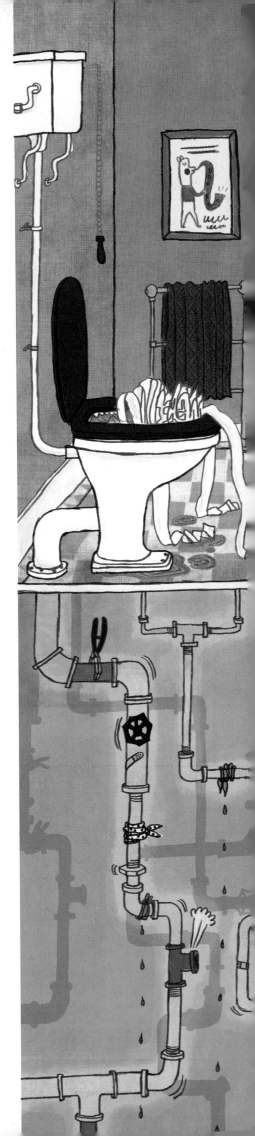

He patched and he botched, he slap-dashed and bungled,

He short-cutted, covered and muddled and fumbled.

No wonder his work was much cheaper and faster!

It was easy to see this would end in disaster . . .

And, sure enough, Croc's pipe sprang a leak,
The pipe that the dog had fixed only last week!

All over Tapton it seemed, one by one,
That Flash Rover's jobs were all coming undone!

"Help!" cried the Mayor. "This dog is a fraud!
As a plumber his work seems disastrously flawed.
His bite was apparently worse than his bark,
We must get some help, or start building an ark!"

BAKERY...

"Tapton is drowning, we're right in a jam,
And no-one can save us but Paulie and Sam!"

Well the two birds were touched by the pleas of the town,
And this was their home - they would not let it drown.

"And really," said Sammy, "that dog is a menace,
For everyone knows this is Tapton, not Venice!"

So they plugged up the leaks and they unclogged the drains,
They cleaned out the pipes: kitchen, bathroom and mains.

They plumbed with aplomb not a second too late,
And rescued the town from a watery fate.

They said to Flash Rover, "You need a new plan,
You CAN'T do the job that the two of us can!
And now that we've cleaned up your mess, you'll agree,
That Tapton just ain't big enough for us three!"

So when the loo's got the blues and the shower's run dry,

When the sink's on the blink and the soap's in your eye.

When the plumbing is driving you round the U-bend,

Who are the twosome on whom to depend?

In Tapton EVERYONE knows who to call,

The toucans that can do – Sammy and Paul!